*Love to Vietnam*

## Books by Edita Morris

# LOVE TO VIETNAM

*a novel by*
*Edita Morris*

CALDER AND BOYARS · LONDON

First published in Great Britain in 1969
by Calder and Boyars Ltd.,
18 Brewer Street, London W1
Originally published in 1968
by Monthly Review Press, New York
© 1968, 1969 Edita Morris

Printed in Great Britain by
Latimer Trend & Co. Ltd., Whitstable

*Part I*

Nagasaki,
February –

Dear Miss Dan Thanh,*

How are you coming ever since? I do hope that your health has improved now.

Oh, I'm twenty-nine years of age, and I work in an establishment that sells film equipment and photographic supplies—the New York Photo Emporium, Inc. That is all there is to me.

If you scrutinize letterhead, you will understand why I wrote you after seeing you on a Vietnam film. Alas, this name stands for more than just name of a city. No one knows as much about burns as we people residing in town on letterhead above. Well, this is enough for today.

I am,
Yours obedient
Nishina Shinzo

P.S. Shinzo is my Christian name. In Japan we put family name first, Christian name second. "Christian" might seem funny to a Buddhist like you, but my town is a Christian town although peculiar thing happened there. All our churches were blown to pieces by the atom bomb in nineteen forty-five, whereas houses of ill-fame in

*In Vietnamese Dan is pronounced *dahn*.

7

Yoshiwara district just across the river remained intact, which painfully surprised friends of Gentle Jesus, who is our patron saint.

N. S.

Nagasaki,
February –

Dear Miss Dan Thanh,

How do you do? Yesterday I failed to tell you *why* I met you on a film, which is peculiar, as I never go to the movies. Well, Issa, a young producer whom my firm deals with commercially, invited me to view a film he took in Vietnam. When I shook so much I couldn't get up after the performance, he said, sit still and take your time. Why did Issa say this? Well, he had taken a look at my physiognomy, a replica of napalmed girl he had used as fade-out in his film. In fact, you, Miss.

"I knew that girl in a hospital in Vietnam," Issa said, which made me shake some more, but then Issa and I went out and had some ice cream together.

"Man, why don't you write to Miss Dan Thanh? It'll cheer her. Just chit-chat! I shall return to Vietnam to take more films, and will deliver your letters."

"When, please?" I demanded.

He retorted: "Why, in a fortnight."

"It's a deal," I answered, which is an expression I've heard in the movies. It is used to end conversations.

Well, if I succeed in selling my nature photos, I shall purchase a better English-Japanese dictionary to improve my schoolboy English. Now I have only a business correspondence textbook which I picked up in second-hand

9

book store, not so good. Miss, since I saw the film with you on it, I'm alert for news from your country. (This is rare for me, who am *outside* of everything.) I know, for example, about Lazy Dog bomb, and I shake.

Assuring you of my best
attention, I am
Nishina  Shinzo

P.S. Have you any skin at all on your right side? After the A-bomb I had no skin on my left side at all. A tree needs its bark!

Dear Miss Dan Thanh,

It is a pleasure to renew our correspondence. Well,
I know more about you and Vietnam than I did yesterday, and will endeavor to tell you why in my thin
vocabulary.

Issa-san turned up. He is a funny customer, which
is a pun. I mean he is actually our customer, but "funny
customer" means a fellow of unusual appearance as well.
His eyes blaze, and he wears his hair cut round like a
Japanese doll.

"Someone to see you," said our office boy, amazed.
For no one ever comes to see me.

"Ha, who?" I asked this of our office boy, peering
up at him with my right eye, for I keep my left side
toward the wall for personal reasons.

Indeed, who could it be? I know no one. (As we were
so unlucky to be here August ninth, nineteen forty-five,
many people think we might bring them bad luck, too.
For this reason they avoid us.) Oh yes, I know my landlady very well. Could it be she?

"It's a tall man with hair like a baby-doll's, Nishina-
san," replied said boy.

So Issa and I had ice cream together in the very dark
ice-cream parlor I patronize, and he told me to call him

"Issa" which is the name of a great Japanese poet who lived among the people, and on whom he models himself. It was good that we'd come to my dim ice cream parlor, for Issa asked:

"Have you seen the evening paper?" showing me a row of humans who looked like burned slices of bacon. "Dan's right side is napalmed like that," Issa said, adding, "They have maimed thousands in a similar fashion in Vietnam, and by 'they' I mean the American government, not the American people." Then he murmured, "Don't bother to finish your ice cream. The toilet is over there. Run! Just vomit!"

Well, today I haven't been back to my office, but they are used to that from my kind, which is the reason they claim we're unemployable. Especially my Senior Clerk, a man filled with worms of venom, makes the claim. This good-looking gentleman hates me. On which note I terminate, and sign myself,

Yours obedient,
Nishina Shinzo

P.S. The moon has grown rounder. Look at her. It will solace you.

Dear Miss Dan Thanh,

How do you come since then? Better-worse? All burns are unpredictable, but please hang on. Insanity is most to be feared, so when your screaming sounds insane, stop!

"Hallo!"

This was Issa's word when he arrived unannounced last night, causing me to take refuge in my darkroom. Reason for flight? He wasn't alone. His hefty girlfriend, who had bleached hair hanging over her face, made me tremble until I noticed her slant eyes. I had mistaken her for a 100 percent American! (Actually she is half and half.) But she might have been all American to judge from the unceremonious way she asked who were the people on my family altar.

"My Honorable Father, my Honorable Mother," I retorted, bowing to that pretty couple.

"That adorable little boy? Who is he?" she asked, pointing to a photo beside them. "Why, it's *you!*" she cried. "But you aren't—dead, are you? Then why is your photograph on the family altar?" "Shut up, please," snapped Issa, who knows that many of us atom-bomb ghosts consider ourselves dead, hence belong on altars.

13

His girl-friend's eyes had melted, water spilled forth. I hurried into my darkroom for I can't bear pity.

"I dropped in to fetch you for an anti-war meeting nearby. Coming, man?" asked Issa who learned that word "man" in a village located in the city of New York. But I shook my head. What use are peace meetings? Besides, being a ghost, I keep myself out of life entirely.

"He's a wise fellow," the mademoiselle, who wore a mini-skirt, told Issa. (Mlle Michiko Dupont is her name. She is a French-American-Japanese born in Louisiana, never been in Japan before. She lives in above-mentioned village in New York, where everyone calls her mademoiselle—written Mlle.) "Anyone who works against the war in Vietnam is bound to lose his job in an American-owned firm like this New York Photo Emporium," she said.

"So what? I lost mine," remarked Issa.

"Yes. I suppose that's why we can't marry," joked bulky Mlle, scratching her beatnik hair with a piece of candy she held in her hand. But Issa, who was peering at some negatives developing in my sink, had turned green.

"Sayonara!" he said, and hurried off, pulling Mlle with him. Oh I don't dare tell you, Miss, what was developing in my sink. Wishing you "sayonara" too, I remain,

Yours obedient,<br>Nishina Shinzo

Dear Miss Dan Thanh,

How do you do? I realize you seldom sleep, but try not to twitch all night. This is frequent with burn victims and paves way to fatal nerve ailments, which we in city on letterhead above know only too well.

This morning three little mice trotted into the kitchen of my landlady, but as my landlady is dim-sighted, which is the reason I chose to lodge with her, she didn't shoo them away. Hence I snapped them with the pocket camera I always carry. For they looked like small, starving men in search of food in your hungry country, which is constantly in my thoughts these days.

I am very fond of animals. They can't laugh at one up their sleeves. I am fond of trees for the same reason, and this morning I snapped the young cherry tree in my landlady's garden in order to add it to the nature-album which I am preparing. My boss opined that said album might win me an Honorable Medal in photography contest. I hope so, although it's unseemly for someone dead to hope.

During the night I dreamed I was married to the cherry tree. You know, she is blooming for the first time this year. We were so happy in the moonlight, I with my head in the arms of her tender branches. Miss, we burnt people pine for love, and would forgo food, if someone would love us.

But later in the day my bliss vanished. I never bother to read newspapers, for we in Nagasaki know what wicked silences they kept about *us* in nineteen forty-five. (Occupation Forces clamped on a strict censorship, allowed no mention of atom bomb casualties in print or in speech, not wishing people to know we were just laboratories of death.) In this war, there is a different policy. They admit everything, even *boast,* and as I passed a newspaper stand this morning, I saw screaming headlines: "Nature devastation in Vietnam to be escalated. Many thousands acres of trees defoliated." Oh, it can't be true! I thought. Only pernicious devils could think of such wickedness. But then I reminded myself that man *has* become a pernicious devil, and I asked our Senior Clerk permission to leave early as I felt sick. Once back home, I leaned against my cherry tree, vowing to protect her against aforementioned devils.

Miss, I can't continue this letter because of my inability to hold my pen. Sometimes I feel I can't go on. Yes, sometimes I feel I can't go on. Luckily I have a pill I can take if I get too desperate. She's sewed into the lining of my pocket. I call her My Pill.

Gracefully accept respectful<br>compliments<br>Nishina Shinzo

Nagasaki,
February –

Dear Miss Dan Thanh,

How are you? This is the correct way of opening a letter in English, I have learned. Please forgive my previous bad ways. Well, Mlle turned up. I hurried towards my darkroom, but she followed me in hot pursuit. She clasped her large hands admiringly before photos which I had snapped of my cherry tree. If they should decide to spray our trees one day there will exist photos to show what our earth looked like before it became one brown scar.

"You're in love with that little tree!" exclaimed Mlle. Then she said something strange: "So *that* is how a cherry tree really looks? I hadn't known it." Quickly she added: "Your eye for detail shows you're a genius for Crissake." Oh, I blushed with pleasure.

But I had nothing to say to this alien beatnik with her swear words and hair falling before face.

"How is Issa?" I asked.

"Oh, rushing about pulling strings."

"Please?" I demanded.

"Trying to get together money to return to Vietnam. Do you hate war as madly as Issa does?"

*Hate war!*

I could not discuss that crime with an outsider who

never had suffered from war, so I turned my left side to the wall and did not answer. When I was young I didn't speak for months sometimes! Now I often don't speak for weeks. But silence was getting too thick.

"Issa . . ." I began again, for fact is that Issa is all we've got in common. "I wish Issa was more like you," murmured Mlle, coming closer. "You speak and move as softly as a ghost, as if you didn't want anyone to notice you. I like that. Issa's leaving in two days' time. Let's meet, you and I."

Two days! That franticked me. Miss, I haven't written to you of my childhood days yet, and now Issa flies off to Vietnam, bringing you my letters without this important explanation of self. I haven't even told you about That Day! I pined for Mlle to leave so that I could write you, hence I begged her to stay. We are taught politeness in Japanese schools, which is really a form of not being unkind. I hate unkindness more than poison.

"Do remain, Mlle."

"No, I've got some errands to make," this kindly lady lied, realizing that my invitation sounded hollow. (She has a little gap between her front teeth: sign of a good heart.) She clattered away on her big Western feet, making my bamboo walls shake. Now I am kneeling before my writing tablet, but before I begin my letter, I must close my eyes to think back on the days when I was still an alive little boy.

Your obedient,
Nishina Shinzo

Dear Miss Dan Thanh,

Well, on That Day I hopped ahead—in front of Mother-Father, I mean—on our way to church. As a boy of eight I was very fond of Gentle Jesus, a corker of a man, and I held a flower in my hand to give to that nice fellow.

*Was* I a gay boy? Oh, yes! Miss, I never stopped laughing throughout my childhood days, and I had two little pits in my cheeks, laughing-pits. Mother-Father, whom I thought of as one person, smiled as I hopped on one leg down our tree-lined street.

"Funny one, stop clowning. We're on our way to church, you funny little boy!"

I hopped on. There lay our church. In the square outside it, five of my school mates kneeled in a ring, playing the Bean Game, and I called out to them, "Hello, Yoshi! Hello Eiichi! Hello, Koichiro, Yuki and Hanno. I'll join you after we come out from church," I said, waving to them with my flower. I gave an extra skip, for I was so happy at the thought that I'd be playing with my friends after having been to church, which I loved, with Mother-Father whom I loved. But just then something hit me. . . .

(Sorry but I had to stop here for some hours which is the reason writing will look different at the beginning of my letter than at the end, which I am about to start with new ballpoint.)

Well, there I lay on the street. I didn't know what had hit me. "What hit me, Mother-Father?" I cried, and I craned my neck to look for them, but they weren't there. They just weren't there, they just weren't there, they just weren't there. . . .

I shouted to one of my five friends in the Bean Game ring: "Yoshi, where did my mother and father go?" The bean players were still sitting in a ring, but they were gazing into the sky, and they did not move or answer me. They were dazed. In fact all had gone blind from atomic flash, as was discovered later. None of them quite recovered their sight, with following consequences: Yoshi has become a jailbird because of his robberies. Hanno is a drunk. Hundreds in our city are now criminals through despair.

A pain started in my left side. I began to scream. I don't know if I screamed for my parents who seemed to have turned into dust and whirled away, or because my left side was raw flesh. Suddenly I felt hungry. I ate up Gentle Jesus's flower. Then I began to scream again, calling in turn for Mother-Father or Yoshi. Later I just screamed, screamed. Well, that was That Day.

Obediently yours,
Nishina Shinzo

Dear Miss Dan Thanh,

How are things? I wish I could send you anti-histamine medicine for your infected burns, but I hear that packages never arrive. Yes, we too, had no medicines in nineteen hundred forty-five. And then, as now, no one cared.

Issa is leaving in a few days. If only I were a butterfly and could ride on his shoulder to Vietnam and you! "If wishes were horses beggars wouldn't walk." This quotation from the British language sounds wrong to my Japanese ears, but let it go.

"Someone to see Nishina-san!" To avoid jeering glances I have placed my desk in the darkest corner of our office, so I didn't notice if our office boy was ogling my keloids as usual. "A man with a round hairdo?" I inquired. "A lady with a straight one," answered the office boy, called Y . . . , whose name I don't like to write as it was the name of my favorite chum in the Bean Game. Our office boy almost collapsed when I laughed. He'd never heard me laugh before. "Shall I show her in?" he asked, but no such formality was necessary.

"I brought my camera. Come on out, Shinzo! I'll show you a new type of photographing," Mlle shouted at the top of her voice, Western style. The colleagues in my room gazed at her admiringly. Heavens, I rose in their low esteem of me. "We'll go downtown and photograph *objects*," Michiko Dupont commanded, but I retorted, "No!" and led her down the deserted alleys I frequent so as to shun people. I even walk with my face so sharply turned leftward that a sinew in my neck has grown askew, which can't be cured, and which adds to my odd appearance. Luckily Mlle liked my alleys, and gave a shriek of joy. For there lay a squeezed lemon in the sand, with an empty saké bottle half buried beside it! She pulled out a roll of toilet paper and, throwing said roll next to these "objects" clicked her camera.

"See?" she asked. I derogated her: "Bosh! Pop art!" giving scornful shrug.

"There's nothing bosh about pop. Pop art's still *in*," cried hefty Mlle while I snapped a delicate bird. (Alas, today's headlines announced that animals are fast disappearing in your burned-up land. Buffaloes are murdered by thousands and young elephants and silky monkeys are all vanishing. Also little singing birds like this one I snapped, I reflected unhappily.)

"For Crissake what came over you?" asked the pop photographer, but as I wear dark spectacles to avoid people's cruel glances, she didn't notice my tears. Even if no people got crucified, destruction of animals, nature, is sufficient to make one lower one's eyes in shame. Please, Miss Dan Thanh, give my love to Vietnam!

Obediently yours,

Nishina Shinzo who sends you
his tears.

Dear Miss Dan Thanh,

How are you feeling tonight? In your head, your heart? I have decided to take another road to my office in order to avoid that newspaper stand with its headlines. "Hundred thousands Vietnamese children have been napalmed to date," it screamed this morning, so I'll take the longer road to my work. (I don't want to get reminded. I remember enough without being reminded.) Luckily I had such a busy day doing invoices that I had no time to think during work hours.

Now it is middle of the night. Miss, at night my brain is a humming factory over whose machines I have no control. Dreams fling me about. Today's headline made me start nightmaring about my own childhood. If a keloid victim has a mother's soft breasts between which he can hide his monstrous face, he may survive emotionally. My mother was blown to pieces, hence I didn't survive, which is the reason I've placed that photo of myself on the altar next to my dead parents. For I, too, died That Day. Yes, emotionally I am dead, which I have never confessed to anyone before. But you are a burnt one too, a napalmed one.

As I said, I dreamt about my childhood, my school in particular. After a long time in gray hospitals I was sent to school, but I had missed so much time that I was put in a class with mere tots, a fresh humiliation. Did these totties torture me? Yes! That is the reason that I have begun to shed drops of sweat on my letter-paper, please excuse them.

In my first little school, classmate Hoko (a future general, maybe, or politician?) emitted ear-splitting atom-bomb noises in order to make me scream and take shelter beneath my desk. This made everyone in the classroom howl in laughter. I was transferred to another school, for one cannot stop the Hokos of this world from tormenting others; one can only remove their victims.

Oh yes, the childhood days of a gargoyle are very bad, so I have got an idea. As they have got into the habit of removing entire populations into Strategic Hamlets, couldn't someone persuade them to build special "hamlets" in which hideous napalm-victims could be stored? No, it's too painful to think of man-made Vietnamese gargoyles. I must stop before I *cannot* stop, which is when my nerves take over.

Sweet Miss, I'll go out and seek solace from my cherry tree, a mere child herself. She looks very frail in the moonlight. She wants me to put my arms around her slender trunk. Oh, I pine to put my unwanted arms about some one frail who wants them.

I remain,

Your respectful servant,

Nishina  Shinzo

Nagasaki,
February –

Dear Miss Dan Thanh,

How do you make out? Please eat some solid food, if obtainable. Do! I subsisted on liquids for years because of my scorched mouth. Result? I look thin as a pencil still. A short pencil moreover, one that has been frequently sharpened.

At dawn a thunderous noise made me leap from my mat with my hands over my ears. Noises are my worst enemies. Are they yours, too? But it was only Issa on his motor bike.

"Give me Dan's letters, man. I'm on my way to the airport. I'll be seeing her for sure, and plan to bring her your missives, also some fine antihistamine medicine for her infected burns."

Oh, what sparkling news! Now you will get well, Miss, all healed, if you persevere. Well, Issa got off his motor bike and was about to lean it against my cherry tree, when I shouted, "No!" and he sent me one of his sharp glances. I looked away. He must have understood how much I love said tree! Well, the sun rose. It made the cherry blossoms on my tree as pink as a girl's cheeks, and Issa's grim face grew dreamy. Then he glanced resolutely away, having no time for dreaming. He stowed your letters, which I had fetched, into the pocket of his black leather jacket and jumped back onto his bike.

"Can't stay! Man, you gave me a valuable idea the other night. I saw what you were developing in the sink in your darkroom," Issa said, and the right side of my face blushed. (The left part can't blush. I can prick it with a pin, but it is as insensitive as a fish bought at fish shop.) "As I was saying," cried Issa, "those enlarged color photos of your own keloids decided me to concentrate on filming people with burns when I'm in Vietnam this time. You'll see, *they* intend to use napalm on all people who don't want to be policed in their Asian empire. That's why you and I must specialize in photographing burns, and get those photos widely circulated to inform innocent people in Asia (and elsewhere) what they are up against from now on," Issa cried, adding: "Man, please take snaps of keloid victims here while I'm away. Dozens of them! Urgent!"

"Not *I!*" I cried hotly.

Oh, Miss, I have never mixed up in anything, nor will I ever do so. I am dead. I exist solely on the photo of an eight-year-old boy on the altar beside my gone-forever parents. I couldn't tell this to Issa, though. He is too devoted to his mission. Issa did not insist. That rare fellow didn't even look disgusted with me, just disappointed. He cried, "Sayonara," and puffed off to the airport.

I ran into the house. I gazed at my just-developed

art-photos which decorate the walls of my dark-room, and again I said "No!" to Issa's suggestion. Then I dipped my latest photograph, "The Waves," into the bath in my sink, and I stood watching the waves ripple out. They soothed me a little. It was still early morning, so I slid back in between my sheets. Sleep is all I want: the sleep of death. (Oh, I told you about The Pill, didn't I? Scarcely a day passes without my considering idea of using said pill.)

Yours obedient,
Nishina Shinzo

Dear Miss Dan Thanh,

Funny to think that pal Issa may actually be sitting beside your bed in hospital, talking away. (I realize "hospital" is only rough shed, and "bed" is a mat on the ground. So sorry!) Your left side looked beautiful on that photo made of you by Issa on his last visit. Vietnamese people are like dainty little trees. Well, maybe you're getting beautiful on your right side, too? I mean, perhaps napalm burns are less deep than keloids, which were *planned* to disfigure one for life.

Well, I've settled down to a sort of peculiar friendship with Mlle. It has changed my colleagues' superior attitude toward me. Iwara-san, our senior clerk, asked for her address, and as I complied, he has ceased torturing me with his quips. He actually offered me a cigar, which I can't smoke because of my still-sensitive mouth. (This Iwara takes the place of Hoko, the tormentor of school days. Please refer to my communication of recent date.) All my fellow clerks say that Mlle is "in"—a silly expression used by inarticulates in that village in New York—because she never combs her hair. Her long, bare legs are "in," too, and so is her "mini" clothing. To me she looks dirty and poor, but kind.

As we share interest in photography, we've been

photographing together like Billy Ho (a busy Britisher) since Issa flew to Vietnam. I do art photos for the album which my boss hopes to sell for me, while Mlle does her pop photos, i.e. a rotting sardine with her eternal roll of toilet paper used as background. Last evening I photoed a beautiful little hill which she said looked like one breast of a lady. In the center of New York lies this village I keep referring to, whose inmates are crazy about bosoms, and also bottoms, which perhaps is the reason for their name, "hippies." Issa's friend lived in the village for years, and it was there people began to call her Mlle. Now suddenly she threw her arm about me, and it felt as if someone had wound a huge leg about my neck.

"Are we to go on like this, Shinzo?" she asked.

"Please?" I interrogated her.

"Well, squares like Issa bore me. He's so terribly concentrated on a cause. You're an artist. For Crissake, what about it?"

What about it? What about what? I didn't understand, but I thanked her in our Japanese-politeness fashion.

"I'm honored for your friendship, Mlle Michiko Dupont. Do rest assured that I return your esteem."

"That isn't what I meant at all," snapped Mlle, taking her arm from my neck and looking suddenly angry. No doubt I had offended her. Fact is, this well-padded Westerner is hard to accept physically, for like all Japanese I love slight, slender creatures with dark leaves for hair like my cherry tree's. "I shan't be calling for you tomorrow, Shinzo," went on Mlle, her eyes on fire. "I'm off to Nara to photograph some temples upside down. Bye!" she said, and stamped off on her ragged sandals that always fall off.

I crept home and had some cooling raw fish for supper. Miss, I am bad at personal relationships. I have had no practice.

Obediently yours,
Nishina Shinzo

Dear Miss Dan Thanh,

Well, yesterday's unlucky experience with Mlle brought back a day in my life I had thought I would never divulge. Why do I tell you this now? Because I believe you can cure your infected burns and become like others if you unceasingly take medicines brought by Issa. They are producing monsters in Vietnam, just as they did in my Japan—not by accident, *on purpose.* Think of that! And, Miss, please don't become like me.

It was a spring day—ten years ago—and spring in Japan makes one's body sing. Mine sang for Tokie Yamashita, laboratory assistant to Professor Nichiwara, whose utensils I cleaned to make my living. Tokie, I may elucidate, was a fellow atom-survivor. She had been friendly to me, like Mlle, which had gladdened my winter. If only spring hadn't come that year!

"Would you like to listen to some music?" I asked Tokie-san in the lab, making my pocket transistor play, "You're my plum-blossom."

Now this young girl was no unblemished plum-flower. Her arms had some small radiation scars which, I had supposed, was the reason she was so good to me. (At times I'd hoped she had other feelings for me as well!) Anyhow, we harkened to the tune, she smiled,

31

hummed "La-la-la," and I laid my arm about her. I had never touched her before. At this she screamed loudly. Our white-coated professor appeared, took in the scene.

"Aren't you ashamed of yourself, Nishina?" he shouted frenziedly. He even shook his old, veined hand at me. (I learned later that that nasty aged man was having an "affair" with Tokie.) "To think that some-one disfigured like you should entertain amorous thoughts is too—too grotesque," sneered the prof. And so I decided to murder him.

I knew where he kept his poisons, and vowed to drop a pill in his *kuko,* a herb-tea he was in the habit of brewing himself to get virility. "Get out!" he thundered. Which I did! But only after stealing The Pill.

Despair, side by side with love yearning, raged through my spring-heated, eighteen-year-old blood that evening. The moon slid up. I also slid up to a certain kind of house and paid my fee to the Madame.

"Please go upstairs." She smiled.

"Oh, thank you, Madame," I said, bowing.

But, Miss, for the second time that day I was cruelly rebuffed. The young person she had assigned to me let out a yell when I walked through the open *shoji. "Get out!"* she shrieked, giving up her much-needed money rather than be forced to love an atom-bomb gargoyle. It was at that moment that I decided to take The Pill *myself.* I returned to my lodgings like a whirlwind, threw myself onto my straw mat, lifted the pill to my mouth. . . .

But a moth wafted in through my open sliding door. Actually it was Beauty itself! The moth had golden antennae. It had a bit of golden fluff between its lovely dark eyes. It had wings of velvet! And I realized that outside my hideous gargoyle-world existed a world of beauty. My pill-carrying hand sank onto the floor. (It was then that my lifelong adoration of beauty began, the adoration that makes me kneel before a blade of grass.)

And now I reiterate the plea with which I began my letter: don't become like me! We young people can't exist without love, you see. But gargoyles *must* so exist, for no one wishes to see "the grimace of atomic war" nor "the grimace of napalm war." It is very hideous, we must admit. Also it makes people feel uncomfortable, perhaps guilty, especially those whose airmen were compelled to cause said atrocities. (Word "compelled" is important. Individual airmen, soldiers, etc., I do not hate, only their government.) No wonder said government refuses exit visas to Vietnam's disfigured victims. They don't wish the outer world to see what they have done to the most innocent creatures on earth—to its little children and young boys and girls.

> I remain,
> Yours obedient,
> Nishina Shinzo

Dear Miss Dan Thanh,

The month of March and a telegram from Issa arrived today. Now I'll get news from you soon, for his wire from Hong Kong read as follows, quote: Arriving Friday please complete series keloid photos I requested urgent Issa unquote.

Alas, I am disappointing both my friends. The only ones I own! I haven't even begun the photos Issa "requested" as I wish to remain uncommitted, being in effect dead. As for kindly Mlle, I should have shown her my gratitude openly instead of just bowing, Japanese style. Her friendship delights me, and I have caught myself smiling because of it while she's been away in Nara (a rare action for me).

"Ha! Lovers' tiff?" Iwara-san taunted me when I entered our office today. "Your fair lady's deserted you? Staying on in Nara, eh?"

"How come you know?"

"Oh, by little birdie—telephone operator in her hotel, to be exact. Blondie had enough of playing the Good Samaritan, eh?" the good-looking man jeered, eyeing my keloids.

Miss, sooner or later everyone peers at one's weak point. They believe it's unconscious. It is, in my opinion,

conscious sadism (we of the city named above *know*!),
and tears of humiliation ran down my cheeks, dropping
on the invoices on my desk.

"Nara, what a flop!"

Well, there was Mlle's voice like a pistol shot. I
jumped to my feet, but it was at Iwara-san that she
threw her grin. My face would have been lost for good
if unpredictable Mlle had not grabbed *my* arm. "Come
on, Shinzo!" she cried.

"Why did you return so soon?" I asked her on the
street, hoping she would say it was because of our
new friendship.

"Nara was full of American beardies with 'L-O-V-E'
painted on their foreheads and lugging around books
on Zen. That's why I hurried back here," laughed Mlle.

I told her I was grateful for her kindly feeling
towards me, but unfortunately Mlle shook her bleached
hair-mass.

"I met a hippie in Nara who had gone there for
introspection," she told me. "It was he who told me
that I must have thrown myself at your head because
of guilt feelings. You see, all the time that you were
dragging yourself about with your burns, I was doing
the frug in the village, enjoying myself. That American
hippie in Nara said Freud thought pity was crap, and
I'd better eliminate it pronto."

"I must run," I lied. Quickly I added that she'd
have Issa back with her Friday. "He's returning from
his mission," I told her, which called up a laugh.

"Issa and his missions! Freud says missions and causes are crap, too. No, it's Iwara-san for me! Do you know, that guy phoned my hotel every day while I was away. So long, Shinzo. See you," she cried in her happy-go-lucky way.

But I stood and shook. Oh, I contemplated swallowing The Pill, the first step of mine into the world of non-burned people having proved a failure. Instead I tramped my deserted lanes all night as I've done for years. Miss, Issa *must* bring me the news that your napalm wounds are healing, for I couldn't bear it if you had to tramp lonely lanes at night.

Obediently yours,
Nishina Shinzo

Dear Miss Dan Thanh,

Well, I spent Sunday snapping turtles. Having decided that I was not fit for friendship with normals, I've returned to solitude like many other atom ghosts. I felt safe, yesterday, lying beneath a weeping willow whose branches hid me from everyone.

"Nishina-san!"

I peered out from under my leaves, and hello! There was my boss Sunday-strolling with sprightly knees and straight back. Hata-san, manager of the New York Photo Emporium, Inc. is crazy about fresh air and exercise.

"Can I share your plot of grass, my boy?" he asked, and kneeled beside me. "Ah! You're photographing a young turtle?"

"No, an oldster, Hata-san. Please note super-wrinkled neck with greenish folds. I have snapped him since 7 A.M.," I informed my Honorable Boss, who remarked that my skill lay in painstaking details.

"I specially admire your close-ups of aged stones," he cried. "A shame that an artist like you must do invoices. But I have hopes of finding a publisher for your nature albums very soon."

"A fish sandwich, please?"

Miss, I was so happy that I had to say something in order to hide my unseemly joy at prospect of a little success (unseemly because I'm dead). We shared my midday meal. While we munched, I told him that I'd studied stones for five years in my orphan asylum.

"No one would play with me, Hata-san. So I sat gazing at everything, which is reason I now comprehend how everything looks," I explained to my fellow luncher.

Then I stopped myself. My boss seemed so interested that his left ear twitched.

"Your story is that of many A-bomb boys," he informed me. "I know what I'm talking about." He proceeded to inform me that he'd lived all his life in Korea, but was forced to return to the homeland with all other Japanese after the war. Like many of them, he came to our demolished city because there was plenty of space there at that time and he built a house among the ruins. (Strange story! I was agog.)

"Well, my boy, one night returning to my domicile, I was set upon by a gang of starved atom-bomb orphans who removed from me everything down to my underdrawers. A policeman joined the fray. Using ju-jitsu, he dispersed the hunger-mad thugs, pummelling their leader, and was set upon by this fellow's pal. Ha! Further policemen and I lugged the wild boy to prison. Can you guess who that tiger was?"

I tossed my head. I am not good at making guesswork.

"Why—Issa!" cried the boss. "Sorry to tell you this. Issa spent thereafter a good many years in jail."

"Jail, oh heavens! What *crime,* please?"

"Oh, murder, please."

Miss, I offered our turtle a morsel of raw fish in order to regain composure. Then, cocking my ears anew, I learned that the dawn when Issa was released, my Boss met him outside the prison gates, and before you could say Jack Robinson he'd offered Issa a job in his small but thriving camera shop. My boss has helped many others since (me included) even after he became manager of the New York Photo Emporium, Inc. But now he's begun to worry about the wild bands of starving Vietnam kids.

"Soon their jails will be filled with child-murderers and hungry thieves, just as happened here. Alas! What an amiss situation. Hop!" cried the boss, who jumped to his feet, and began to do his daily exercises. "One-two-three. Must keep fit to cope with all these troubles. Goodbye!" he cried, and rushed off.

Well, that was my Sunday, Miss. It ended pleasantly enough, for the turtle, with a morsel of raw fish between its teeth, ambled over and rubbed its neck against my sandal. Please find an animal to console you. An insect, even, consoles a lonesomer.

> I sign myself,
> Obediently yours,
> Nishina Shinzo

Nagasaki,
March –

Dan,

You have asked me to call you Dan, and I am inside seventh heaven with thank-you feelings. *Thank you.* (But I must proceed in a chronological fashion, as is advised in my business correspondence textbook. I have now purchased second-hand a book called *Letter Writing Aid,* so shall write you less business-style letters in future.)

Referring back to comunication of 3rd inst., well I *didn't* stick to my resolution not to see anyone and keep to my own company as I've done all my life. For Issa crawled in, breaking my solitude.

"Got some saké, man?"

I was flabbergasted. Pal Issa had become ten years older at least.

"I don't drink," I had to answer him.

"Well, *get* some saké!"

Oh, that would mean that I would be obliged to show myself in neighboring bar. How embarrassing! But one look into Issa's face made me go off running.

"A bottle of saké!" I told the barman.

"Where did *he* come from? A man from the moon?" jeered one of the drunken gentlemen at the bar, peering close at my keloids.

I have always pined to visit this romantic little bar with its blue lantern and haunting *samisen* music. Now what I pined for was to get out! But it took the honorable barman long ages to wrap up my bottle. It seemed ages, I mean.

"I'm back, Issa," I cried.

But where was Issa? Gone off into the night with his wild eyes? A rustling sound sent me into my darkroom, where I uncorked the bottle and held it out to Issa, who was standing gazing at some film he had carried back from his trip. He was developing said film in the sink.

I, too, looked down at it, then put my hand before my mouth. Oh, oh! I choked down a cry, making myself look closer. Those photos were of pretty girls with putrefying napalm sores down their breasts and bellies.

"*Yes,* man. That's it. That's Vietnam! Get drunk, man. Get drunk, I say! My cameraman refused to drink, hence cracked up. He's gone berserk like many, including American soldiers, and I've had to leave him with his family in Tokyo; they're watching him night and day. This guy tries to mutilate himself the way he saw people mutilated in Vietnam. Look at this photo."

I complied.

"Saké, please," I whispered.

Well, Dan, late at night after we'd finished photo development, also the saké bottle, I asked:

"Miss Dan Thanh, please?"

"Asks you to call her Dan, and to continue to write

to her. She likes you and your letters make her feel not so lonesome. 'Shinzo and I have almost the same burns. We are twins. Non-identical twins,' she told me, speaking her school-girl English."

"And her—health?" I whispered.

Issa showed me another negative floating in my sink.

"That isn't Dan?" I shouted.

"No. But it's another girl of seventeen, also recipient of napalm. They have produced tens of thousands of such martyr-monsters in Vietnam to date. Man, don't turn away your head. Look at the photo, man. Hey! Steady! Here! There's a slug left in our saké bottle."

Dan, I stood there looking. That's when I swore never to look away again. Issa said, and I've never heard him speak like that:

"Brother, I shan't leave you tonight. I'll share your mattress with you."

Issa called me brother! *Me?* Goodnight, Dan. Goodnight, twin.

Your Shinzo

Nagasaki,
March –

Dan,

Referring to my communication of recent date re antihistamine, I beg you not to share the supply Issa left with you. One must look out for oneself! Even so it is hard to survive, but once you begin sharing your last button or last antihistamine pill, you are lost. And you *must* get your burns cured, Dan! Why? Well, in the city named above lots of survivors can not find jobs because of hideous disfigurement, hence live like pigs in shacks, subsisting on—well, I shan't tell you what they still subsist on, twenty-two years after holocaust.

I couldn't concentrate thoughts on my invoices today. I sat with my head in my hands, and my fellow-clerks sniggered among themselves, thinking I mourned Mlle Michiko Dupont, whom our Honorable Chief Clerk keeps taking out for dinner at the Pink Dragon. Strange to say, I didn't mind their taunts. Something happened to me last night when I looked at the devastation of your country.

"Nishina-san!"

Dan, I jumped to my feet. Our Boss, Hata-san, he who gazed at that ancient turtle in my company last Sunday, was addressing me. I bowed to him.

"I'll give you one more chance, Nishina-san," he

told me, while all cocked their ears. "My Senior Clerk has just informed me that you absent yourself too often. No doubt you feel unfit, but I can't have you sit idling with your head in your hands."

This all, I later understood, he was saying for the benefit of my fellow-employees. But then he lowered his voice so that they wouldn't hear.

"I know your situation, my boy. Ah, the atom bomb hasn't done with you people yet! You are invalids. You were meant to survive in said state as example of what awaits other people who refuse to submit. Ha! You A-bomb victims are just guinea pigs, no more," he said. "New guinea pigs are needed, now that you A-bomb invalids are old hat. Napalm is a new weapon, easy to use. They believe they can frighten all Asians, and gain economic control. Hence the Vietnam war."

Then Hata-san got control of himself. He looked around. Blinking his tiny scared eyes, he spoke to me loudly, angrily, for benefit of the clerks with flapping ears:

"Nishina-san, we must have an A-1 efficiency office here. After all, this is the branch of an American firm. No nodding on the job. In America they have the smooth society, everything working like oil. For that reason USA now is great democracy of the West which we all look up to—and *love!*" shouted Boss, and again his nervous eyes swept over the listening clerks. "America is a fine Christian country," he cried. "So long!"

The small fellow closed the door behind him. His

44

exit was followed by exchange of glances between some of the clerks. I'm afraid he had not convinced them and that they would all put their heads together like players in a football game, conspiring against him. Dan, they don't like softhearted Hata-san, who employs people like me that lower the prestige of the office. (They would be happy to get something on him to pass to higher authorities.)

I plunged into my invoices, vowing to work late every night in order to show appreciation to my boss to whom I'd give my right arm because he feels deeply about martyred people, here and in your country too— your Vietnam to which I send my love.

Remaining yours confidentially,
Nishina Shinzo

Dan,

"Why, *you*!" I cried, yesterday.

"Who else?" snapped Mlle, shuffling into my dim ice-cream parlor on her straw sandals. "I knew I'd find you here," she said, dumping herself onto the tatami upon which I kneeled before a pecan ice cream.

"Same, please?" I asked.

"No, a sherbet. I'm putting on weight on account of your goddam rice. Say, what's the matter with Iwara-san? He's the reason I've tracked you down in your ice-cream lair today. Goddamit, I shall never see him again. Does he think I'm a geisha, or what? I mean, the way he treats me?"

"Honorable geishas are very respectable, cultured young ladies," I answered coolly, wishing that Mlle's legs weren't exposed almost to her hip, causing the eyes of our sherbet-bearing waiter to protrude from their eye-holes.

"And I am *not*? Your fellow-clerk propositions me as if I were a - a . . ."

"Pam-pam?" I suggested.

"What's that, for Crissake?"

"A word dating from World War Two. Starving Japanese teen-age girls did anything for condensed milk.

The G.I.'s and their officers turned occupied Japan into one big brothel, same as Vietnam today. You see, Issa has returned. And he told me about the happenings in Vietnam," I began, but Mlle interrupted me, as is evidently the custom of Western ladies.

"So the Crusader's back, is he? He certainly hasn't contacted *me*," she cried, and then she added: "Well, for Crissake go on! What happened to your pam-pams?"

"Babes! Now these mixed-blood babes are all grown up, and shunned by Westerners, also by Japanese, which accounts for the hair-raising suicide rate among them, also hair-raising crime rate and other hair-raising rates among those now-adult G.I. babes. The same will happen in Vietnam in twenty years, only more so, as hunger in Vietnam is even worse than it used to be here, and many teen-age Vietnamese girls are orphans," I answered Mlle, whose nice eyes showed sadness.

"Vietnamese pam-pams, eh? Like *me*? Oh, I do sleep around a lot, I admit. What's the harm? Anyhow, what's a girl to do? Holy Crusaders like Issa have got no time for us. And sweet guys like you. . . ."

"Yes, what about me, please?" I asked, afraid she'd refer to my scars. This she did promptly.

"Well, my psychoanalyst once told me not to work off my guilt complex on—unfortunate people," retorted Mlle, who by now had eaten all of my pecan ice cream, as well as her own sherbet.

Psychoanalyst? Quickly I edged away from her.

"You have been—crazy, then?" I asked Mlle, whereupon she clattered to her feet. "No, but I will get crazy if I talk to you any longer. Don't you know *anything*? All women in my country get psychoanalyzed for Crissake," she snapped. But then she regretted this outburst and sad look referred to above returned to her eyes.

"I've turned into a bitch, haven't I? Oh, Shinzo, I'm unhappy—unhappy inside, like most females in my sad-mad country," cried Mlle, and I wish I could have taken this unhappy lump in my arms.

Bad luck, she had run off in her rough way. Oh, did she *ever* know what she was doing? Meanwhile my friend, the honorable Ice Cream Waiter whose family, like mine, had been swept away in our holocaust, brought me another ice cream, free of charge, on which note I end, signing myself,

Your Shinzo

P.S. Forgive this chit-chat letter, but Issa told me to entertain you with anything to lessen your pain. (How lightly non-sufferers use said word pain, even Issa!)

Dear Dan,

If your medicine supply becomes low, please drink
fruit juice. Try to catch back your health, or your soul,
like mine, will become crooked. Today, for example,
when I delivered the Vietnamese negatives I'd developed
for Issa, I died a thousand deaths. (Figure of speech.)
You see, people in his crowded office elevator stared at
me. Oh, I know I should not care! My mind is covered
with keloid scars, hence should be as insensitive as my
body wounds have become. It isn't. It whines like a
kicked dog when anyone ogles me.

"Issa, who is that blindfolded, gagged, and labeled
oldster?" I asked my friend, pointing to one of the
photos he'd brought back from Vietnam, and which
I'd developed for him. We were kneeling on a rush-
mat in his modern office where Issa, who has not the
time nor the wish to enjoy comfort, falls down to sleep
at night.

"It's an old man from Dan's district—perhaps someone like her grandfather," Issa retorted and explained
to me that your grandfather had been a peasant, but
your father had been an engineer. "I stress those words
'had been,'" Issa added, "for Dan's whole family was
killed in the war. You are all she has in the world,"

49

Issa said, and my heart began to jump, for *you* are all *I* have in the world! "Is he—dead?" I whispered, pointing to the photo of that venerable aged man, who was trussed like a duck on its way to the market.

"Well, breathing is most necessary for staying alive," answered Issa in the casual tone he uses when most furious. "They often gag people on their way to interrogation centers," Issa explained.

He peered at me to ascertain if I was looking away from the photo as had been my habit. I wasn't. I have sworn (see communication of previous date) never to look away from human tragedy again. Hence I gazed at this honorable grandfather and compared him to *my* grandfather, also killed by *them*.

"Say, Issa, why don't you print an album with Vietnamese victims on one page and Japanese victims on the opposite page, showing sameness of methods used in nineteen forty-five and nineteen sixty-eight? Understand? Both burn-injuries, you see. Is mine an O.K. idea? A Vietnam-Japan album, so to speak."

"Very O.K.! The album is splendid. Also a film, perhaps," cried Issa and jumped to his eager feet. "We'll do it together, man, how's that?"

When Issa said that word "together" something big happened inside me. An alive Shinzo came out of the dead Shinzo! I became at that moment a fellow with a goal.

"Then you must teach me film-taking," I begged,

for I knew only how to use a Nikon 35-millimeter and other types of still cameras.

"Right away!" Issa promised. "You're a talented photographer. You will learn the art of filming with no difficulty."

Well, we worked for hours. During the evening I asked Issa what is talent, and he retorted as follows: "Talent is passion—a sort of passion." Then he flopped down on his rush mat and snored. But he woke up almost at once. "Fetch me tomorrow before office work, at dawn," he exclaimed. "We'll go to the back streets where the atom-bomb ghosts live, and shoot film. Our Japan-Vietnam film will be terrific," Issa stated before falling asleep again.

With that word *our* in my ear, I dashed into the streets. Funny, my head was not turned toward the house wall, as was my habit, and my crab-walk was changed. I looked back at the first pedestrian who peered at my keloid scars. This middle-aged female sent me a smile, and my step became lively after making this first good contact with a human on a crowded street. Ha!

On that note I terminate, with respectful thanks to you for needing me, as stated by Issa.

Yours,
Shinzo

Dan,

Title of one of the documentary films Issa brought back from Vietnam was quote *Don't* say "No one told me" unquote. He showed them last night at a small Student Center. If I had seen the above-mentioned film a week ago, I would have sweated, trembled, run home in tears. Now that I am in the fight against wars, I stayed.

Oh Dan, what things they have done to your land! Let me tell you about the film. Well, the first scene was a string of ears decorating the wall of a South Vietnam military installation, with the caption: "This is what happens to patriotic resistance fighters who stand up to foreign invaders." The second scene was crackling villages. The caption read as follows: "They have thrown a million tons of bombs on Vietnam, more than all the tonnage they used on the Nazis in Europe and Africa."

The third scene, a squadron of planes dropping death in some form or other on human beings. Caption said: "Hitler and Mussolini had Spain as their laboratory. American 'hawks' are using Vietnamese as *their* guinea pigs, and have to date created over one million casualties."

Snap! At that moment the electric light in the Student Center gave above sound, and I thought, ha, the performance will be stopped. A loud female voice cried, "I'll mend it. Here I come!" It was Mlle's thunder-voice. By the flashlight I always carry (seeing I follow dark back alleys by preference) I saw her stamping toward the fuse box. What is that hippie doing at this anti-war meeting? I asked myself. Another surprise came and went. In the above-mentioned flashlight I met the eyes of—guess who—my boss!

Oh, Hata-san looked away fast. I too! I knew he wasn't happy to be seen at an action protest meeting like this. (Question: In Japan, and other countries too, are many people feeling as violent as myself about Vietnam war, but don't dare take action, as afraid of losing jobs?) I hoped no spy had seen Hata-san.

The film continued, ending with the head of a sad-looking water buffalo who "told" the audience that eighty thousand water buffaloes—poor Vietnamese peasants' only riches—had been burnt up. Then the show was over and everyone hurried out drying their eyes. Not me, who joined Issa in the back room.

"My new photographer," Issa introduced me, and I let out a happy "Ha!" from joy and surprise. Funny, not one of Issa's anti-war friends looked at my keloids. I was welcomed like a real human being for almost the first time in my life.

After this they talked about Issa's film, and Issa admitted the photography of said film should have been more artistic. His cameraman perhaps was not always up to his scratch. "But I've got a new cameraman now," Issa said, and put his arm through mine as we left. I felt like hopping on one leg as I'd done on "the day I died." But I didn't feel like being dead any more. Oh, Dan, we must both of us live! You're only seventeen, a schoolgirl. I too am not aged. Have we Asians no rights, except the right to die?

Your Shinzo

My Dan,

How are you tonight beneath the moon? We talked
of you at dawn today on our way to the film site, in
that part of our town which many jobless atom-bomb
ghosts haunt. Heavied down by film equipment, Issa
marched on, telling me that your honorable family had
farmed near the same village for centuries, but that said
village is now gone—pouff! like my tree-lined street.
Ah, we really *are* twins! Issa also told me that you were
a student, and had saved from the flames a little algebra
book which you love. Dan, we will cure your napalms
and then you will be a student again.

"Good-day," said someone, squatting on a sack.

Issa had wanted to film this squatting keloider, but
now he hesitated. Fact is, Issa is embarrassed that he
escaped (physically) from the atomic holocaust. Reason?
He inhabited a distant suburb. Many escaped survivors
have felt guilty towards their murdered ancestors, though
of course it is not their fault that they're still alive,
although dead inside.

"May I film you, please?" I asked above-mentioned
fellow on his sack. After I had explained the purpose
of our movie, he retorted: "Yes please!" As other survivors crept out of their rabbit holes, carrying water

pots to fill at the well, Issa suggested, "Let's call our film *A quiet day in hell.*" He told me to ask my fellow-keloiders to continue their daily jobs; example: sweeping, carrying, cooking rice, etc. I followed them about with Issa's 16-millimeter movie camera.

Ah, Dan, how I hated those who had ruined these people's faces and lives! I understood what Issa meant when he said that talent was a sort of passion. I shook with anger. Well, I guess I had grown pale as I filmed huge scars that looked like valleys on the moon. When I had finished, the first keloider we'd spoken to said, "You're green, have some hot rice soup in my shack before you leave." "Ha, thank you," I answered. The soup was mostly water, but it was hot. I gulped same.

"Look! What's behind that curtain?" Issa asked as a small sound floated to our ears, and our honorable host, Abe-san, closed his eyes. Then he opened above-mentioned eyes.

"Little moans come from my daughter. Bad luck, she is disfigured completely. As you know, many women were pregnant when A-bomb dropped down on them, and thereafter gave birth to monster-children. Our daughter has sat for twenty-two years behind that partition because not suitable to look upon."

Abe-san said all this in a whisper. Thereupon strong Issa laid his head in his hands, and didn't move.

"Good-bye, Abe-san," we said after a while, and I felt most close to the old man as we bowed farewell.

Why had I fled from my fellow-keloiders so long? Why had I lived among hostile non-sufferers? Answer: I had not made the decision to fight those who had ruined us, hence had kept away from these people's suffering.

We bowed again. "Come back!" cried our host. "I will," I retorted.

Well, Dan, the day passed quiet at the office, but soon after I returned to my lodging in the evening the honorable barman arrived from his bar next door.

"Urgent phone call!" he cried.

"For *me*?" I interrogated, for I never get a phone call.

Soon over the wire I heard Issa's voice, like a shout.

"Man! I've had parts of today's film developed. It's stupendous! Wow! You have talent, man. Goodbye."

Well, Dan, I spent the night beneath my cherry tree in whose branches stars seemed to hang. I whispered to her, to my tree, "I am happy."

Dan, I am happy,
Shinzo

Dan,

On the 15th instant in the morning my fellow clerks started gleefully hammering on their desks when I entered, singing, "Sa-yo-na-ra! Sa-yo-na-ra, Ni-shi-na-san!" I didn't know what they meant, but shot a look toward the Boss's office, afraid that he would hear that unseemly din.

"Don't hope for protection! Even Hata-san can't help employees of the New York Photo Emporium who attend anti-war meetings," sneered our Senior Clerk. Sauntering to my desk, he pointed with an insolent forefinger: "You're out, peacenik! Read letter of dismissal on your desk," he commanded, which I did.

"Who gave me away?" I raged.

"Look who's puffing himself up!" Our Senior Clerk blew rude smoke in my face. "Your pam-pam spilled beans when she was drunk, and I dispatched information to Interested Quarters. Thanks to *me,* the intelligence service knows all about you," he boasted, and I noticed that this unsavory individual wore a new suit, new tie, new suede shoes. I swiftly put together two and two. "I've got rid of your pam-pam as well," bragged that hateful natty dresser.

"*She* got rid of *you,*" I retorted, gathering the

belongings on my desk, especially the beloved stone I found in holocaust-ruins and use as paper weight. "Mlle Michiko Dupont is a *nice* woman. Sayonara," I said, and left—for where? Oh, naturally for Issa's office, since I am now penniless.

However, a little message protruded from his typewriter, informing me that Issa had flown on a lightning mission to Vietnam and would be gone one week. I was dismayed. What should I do with myself? Well, to begin with, I cleaned up Issa's mouse-trap office and sharpened all his pencils. (I love pencils, especially Faber No. 2.) Then I awaited the next day, when I'd start job-chasing—a hopeless hunt no doubt because of my face.

I was hungry, so I nibbled on my fingers, remembering my former unemployed, finger-chewing periods. I washed down my meal with water. Soon I shall stretch out on Issa's rush mat to think of you on *your* rush mat, beside which lucky Issa may be kneeling at this minute.

On which note I terminate.
Your Shinzo

P.S. Permit me to whitewash Mlle whom I judged unfairly. How come, I asked Issa the other day, how come that poor-looking Mlle who drinks, fools with men, speaks hippie-nonsense, etc. attended our serious anti-war meeting?

"Mlle is neither poor nor unserious," Issa stated,

adding the following: "Mlle Michiko Dupont dresses like a tramp because she is acting out the part of a Greenwich Village inhabitant. She drinks lots, I admit. She sleeps around lots, also admitted, and she talks hippie-talk because she's an uncultured drop-out. They all of them conform to this style, because they wish to 'express' themselves, hoping to acquire a personality, which they don't have. Anyway, many of these kids, like Mlle, have well-off parents. How else can they afford to loaf, drug, drink, and then cover their faces with messy hair, which makes a decent job impossible?" Issa stopped and grinned. "Mlle *must* put on a show, or die from boredom," he cried. "But she's a good kid."

Oh, Dan!

Kindly note that a short time only has passed since my letter, yet I've lived through a long stretch of pain. Issa told me the news. To bomb a hospital! To do it wilfully, planned out, as was no doubt the case! No four-footed dog would do such a cruel thing, only *man*. Issa says that if Vietnamese friends had not helped him he could not ever have found your present shelter. He said you looked so beautiful lying on your straw mat with your long hair spread about, that he took a shot with quick-speed panchromatic film type xx, but the light was bad. Result not very good. I can make out on print your figure on the mat, with a book lying beside you. (Is it the algebra book you like so much?) How horribly crowded this shelter, where you and fellow survivors were carried from the bombarded hospital! Issa said also that your infected napalm burns are *not* getting well. This is bad news indeed.

Well, I ran out in the streets after Issa had fallen asleep at midnight, for the long trip had exhausted him. My feet took me to the part of town where Issa and I had filmed, and I stamped the narrow lanes between shacks of unemployed atom-bomb survivors, listening to their sighs and thinking of you and your sleepless nights. And I swore that I would never stop talking, filming, fighting, to make them stop bombing your country, producing each day burn victims like those people in your shelter. Ah, Dan, I'll write to kings and millionaires about your burns. "H-E-L-P, kings! H-E-L-P, millionaires!"

At dawn I made my way back to Issa's place, and by lucky chance, I passed my own lodgings. Ha! There stood the tree! In pink morning light a breeze stirred her long branches. What did they look like? I asked myself this question. Yes, like *your* hair in photo, spread over the straw mat! I cried out with joy then. So my beloved cherry tree and you were in some way the same thing. In loving my cherry tree I had all this time loved *you*, Dan! I whispered: I love you. I love you. Yes, now I have decided following: I will go to you, even if I have to *swim* to Vietnam.

Shinzo

Dan,

A single-minded young man is a bulldozer, no obstacles exist for him. Even money obstacles get pushed aside and job comes his way.

"I'm hiring you as my permanent camera man from today," Issa announced to me. "I shall pay you a monthly, but not a princely, salary and you can sleep in my office. That way we can work on our burns-photos night as well as day." To which I answered the following:

"Yes, Issa, we must. They have already begun to napalm-bomb in South America, using South American pilots to do the dropping of said bombs on guerrillas. Soon South American boys and South American girls —like Dan—will writhe from maggot-infested burn-wounds. I didn't sleep all night from reading about this new horror. We must sure hurry up with our burn-film."

"Agreed, but on a shoestring, man!" Issa answered. "Funds are running very low."

I asked: "Where to find above-mentioned shoestring, please?"

Issa stood scratching his round hairdo, worried. I gave a shout. "Mlle! Her father was a wine dealer, made dough out of Bordeaux. Said father's widow is well off, so I'll squeeze Bordeaux-dough out of Mlle. I'm off!" I cried, which made Issa give a shout of laughter. "Say, you've changed, man!" he cried.

I laughed, too, but just then a severe stomach cramp cramped me. "No, I can't take your cameraman's job away from him," I stated. "Even if I am better photographer, like you say." Upon which Issa informed me: "Easy, man! My camera fellow is done for, sorry to say. The stepped-up bombing on our last trip with resulting mass-casualties cracked him. He hadn't been trained to take 'mechanized' brutality," Issa explained.

Mlle called "Come in," when I tapped at her hotel room. There she sat nude by the window, just going to drop a used-up brassière in the waste basket. Ha! A real hippie, that fat girl, Michiko Dupont! When she saw who it was her big mouth sort of came apart. I thought she was going to weep.

"For Crissake, I know it's my fault that you got kicked out of your job. I didn't realize I'd given away a secret when I spilled beans about that anti-war protest meeting," said Mlle, and suddenly she slapped her mouth hard. "Take *that,* you goddam, drunken mouth!" she cried, then wound, absent-minded, a green bath towel about her bare body. "Oh, I can never make up for what I've done to you, Shinzo!"

"You *can,*" I retorted, pressing home my advantage. "Help pay for Issa's burns-film. Can you let us have a few yens, Mlle?"

Right away that stout, almost-naked girl got busy

looking for something beneath a heap of empty saké bottles. She fished out a check book and scrawled her name with a big sweep on a check.

"A few yens? Crap! This is half my year's allowance. Take it! For Crissake, stop bowing. I can always go to work, I suppose," she said, and suddenly I held plump Mlle in my arms, and she wept like a child. Then she pushed me away, and told me to run out and buy some saké so we could celebrate.

"Celebrate what?" I inquired.

"Isn't that *my* business for Crissake. Scram! Get lost!" shouted Mlle, and suddenly I liked her terribly much. I sang for the first time since I was eight years old as I hopped on one leg down her stairs to get saké.

And now Dan, Dan, I am coming to see you. Yes, for fact, I am coming to Vietnam—to Vietnam to which I send my love.

Shinzo

*Part II*

Dear Mlle,

Now I have on black cotton trousers and a round hat like a wheel. Issa, too, has on black pajamas, so that no one shall note we are not Vietnamese. But Dan "recognized" me right away! (Issa had taken me straight to her overcrowded shelter, which smelled of infected wounds.) She held out her hand, like a circle of cherry blossoms. And we have held hands ever since.

Ah, this sacrificed girl is much more ill than I had thought. Her burned limbs twitch, like mine used to do when I made effort not to scream. This, however, makes her whole body shake, and sweat drops down her face. Today I told her: scream. She did.

Mlle, you said before I flew: "Write me what Vietnam is like." Excuse please, I can't obey. To me Vietnam is this tumbledown shelter which I scarcely leave, filled with limbless bodies, and with voices pleading for death. But Dan and I live on a quiet island—the island of our love. We have already got little "habits" like a married couple. We chat at some hours, doze at others. In the afternoon, when the slanting sun leaves Dan's straw mat, I move the mat, because she, like me, loves sun. We have our own language (school English) and Dan likes when I tell her of our future home in Nagasaki. Our bamboo house on a tree-lined back street will look like my childhood street which was blasted away. I thumbtacked a drawing of above-mentioned house to the wall, and my napalmed girl lies gazing at it, a beating heart in each eye.

Tonight she, Dan, pulled open her torn jacket in a pain spasm. A small tot crawled onto her mat and grabbed Dan's breast with hungry paws. Although no milk *could* come from Dan's virgin breast, the infant fell asleep from the touch of her warm skin. And our eyes met over its head, saying *our* child. It was the first time I've seen Dan truly smile. But then tears poured from her eyes and onto her breast, and the infant drank them, thirsty for liquid. Tears are the milk of the sacrificed Dans of Vietnam.

Well, she dozed off. I stood guard over my little family on our island of love. Busily I switched away flies, I switched away flies! But soon the baby's mouth let go of Dan's nipple, and as I looked closer, I choked a cry in my fingers. Finally I took it away. Mlle, I brought it to the far end of our open shed to bury later. And I became a father as I carried our child's body, whose burned skin, just ash and tissue, came off on my hands and arms. All at once I understood what a father feels. So now I am a father in my soul.

Nagasaki doesn't seem far away any more. My burnt city and Dan's burnt country are twins. Cheek to cheek they mourn like poor twins, the same way Dan and I mourn—cheek to cheek. On this note I end, signing myself,

Yours faithfully,
Nishina Shinzo

Dear Mlle,

What's new with you? Well, over here an American soldier's heart broke in two. Because of seeing what he had seen, he tried to put himself into flames like the Buddhist monks. They hurried the screaming boy away to some veterans' hospital, whose walls are sound-proof, I have been told. Ah, yes, I pity many American soldiers.

"Can you eat a little banana mush?" I asked my Dan yesterday, Mlle. "No," my delicate twig answered with a childish shake of her head. "Then maybe a little fruit juice?" I begged. She nodded, and I shot off for a juicy paw-paw fruit.

The streets were full of bright boys, girls, plus oldsters digging holes into which to jump if a bombing plane appeared. My photographer-eye stored up their faces, which looked prepared for Life and Death alike. Bad luck, that market wasn't full of juicy paw-paws or much of anything, just silent people staring skywards. Now that the enemy has taken over this district, not more than three people are allowed to gather for fear that they might speak against them—and who else would Vietnamese speak against except those who are annihilating them? But just as I had purchased a brightly green lime from a woman who let it go only after she had beheld my scarred face, the marketplace became as a Japanese Kabuki theater. Ha! Who was this gaudily dressed actor who'd bounded onto the stage?

"You speak what language? Some French, a little English?" asked a Vietnamese student. "A little English," I answered absent-minded, for I was already photographing like Billy Ho. Oh, just imagine! That nattily dressed actor was an ape! And his red and yellow costume was covered with anti-war slogans.

"Please *don't* protect us! Please stop doing things for our good! Please cease to send us gifts from heaven! *Please go home!*" was written there.

Everyone applauded, Mlle, and just then the sharp-eyed monkey spotted Dan's green lime in my hand. He snatched it away and swung himself onto a roof, while policemen peppered him with shots for agitating against the war. For answer he threw the shell of Dan's sucked-out lime at above-mentioned police, then disappeared with a grin. All the Vietnamese people in the marketplace giggled.

"Allow me to explain," said my student. "We dress up apes from our jungles and bring them to the cities to spread anti-war propaganda which *we* are forbidden to spread. Awfully splendid idea, or not so splendid?"

"Splendid!" I retorted.

The student gave me a lime he had in his pocket, then looked at my keloids with kindly eyes and murmured: "Where from?"

"Nagasaki!" I told said student.

He embraced me, and I ran back to our shelter, feeling that I loved Dan's countrymen. Dan drank her lime juice. Then she went to sleep with her head resting in my hand.

Goodnight for now, Mlle.<br>Nishina Shinzo

Vietnam,
May –

Dear Mlle,

Have you photographed more temples upside down? Or some sardines with clothes hangers, making pop art picture as you explained? Here pop seems very unreal, most far away.

But Vietnam world is very real. It tries to survive against all obstacles. The people give themselves no rest, just fight and try to build up their courage. Well, look what happened yesterday.

Boom! A Vietnamese gong clanged, and I asked the engineer who lies on a straw mat near Dan and speaks a little English: "More bombers?"

"No. More actors," he said. "A troupe has just arrived nearby. Splendid, not so? Heroic performers will play this evening, though it is forbidden, of course."

Same gentleman regretted his inability to help me carry Dan out to see the spectacle. But, good luck, Issa walked in.

"Man, let's carry Dan out to see *The Sorcerers' Dance!* The Freedom Actors have just set up their stage in the grove, where they won't be spotted." He grabbed Dan's mat and signed to me to seize the other end. "Got her?" he asked.

75

"Got her!" I answered and added, within me: "Forever."

We brought her over to the bamboo grove, also the engineer on his litter, bombed tots as well. The sickest napalmers couldn't be dragged out, for their skin comes off in one's fingers, and they are really dying. The not-so-sick spectators shouted with laughter when the actors put on a drum-and-dance scene, singing: "Ho-he-ho!" shaking their fists at imaginary enemies.

Later, Mlle, these young hero-actors played melodies on traditional Vietnamese string instruments. The engineer explained that they are trying to preserve classical Vietnam-tunes, discouraging frug-swing-pop music, which is fit only for uncivilized people. He said their songs told about ups-and-downs of the country's age-long struggle.

"Many *ups,* despite difficulties," he told me, laughing although he's lost both hands from a fragmentation bomb—one of those terror-weapons they throw at civilians. But *"Down!"* shouted one actor then, and before you could say Robinson they'd put out all their little kerosene lamps.

"Lie flat on your stomach," the engineer translated.

Oh, what had happened, Mlle? Well, a screaming bomber had flown over, and we all lay on the ground, afraid it would send down a bomb by mistake or perhaps for fun. Good luck, the plane flew off soon.

"Ho-ho!" sang the triumphant actors. They laughed and skipped. We applauded: "More! More!"

But Dan was tired. The excitement had been too much for her. Ah, Mlle, my girl gets tired so quickly! Yet her wounds seem better, so I can not understand why she is still so very weak. Time, and my love, will heal her. I was glad when we were finally alone on her mat with the night for blanket. Dan had been so joyous about those young actors' optimism, but now she seemed unhappy, restless.

Finally I said in a resolute voice: "Dan, the Vietnamese people will win—no matter what happens. *They* have lost—whatever happens!"

"Yes," she answered. Then she added the following words in her school English: "You are a Vietnamese now, Shinzo. Aren't you, Shinzo?"

*"I am!"* I cried this so loudly that I'm afraid I woke some sleepers. "The whole decent world is Vietnamese today," I reiterated.

It's true, Mlle. In Japan, in *all* countries, men of heart feel themselves Vietnamese.

Dan gave a satisfied little sigh. But while she fell asleep in my arms, my heart cracked from pity and apprehension.

Remaining yours faithfully,
Nishina Shinzo

Dear Mlle,

We are far apart, but I think of you and wish joy to hurry toward you. Why should it not? You are a generous girl, which means that you are good person. People love those who are good (although they don't know that is the reason). And if one is loved, one is happy. Your hippie friends may scorn this. Let them! Human truths are better than hallucinations by L.S.D.

Well, last night I thought *I* was hallucinating. Three youngsters, victims of anti-personnel bombing, were carried into our shelter, as well as two screaming oldsters. The sixth survivor was a monk who was lowered onto a mat next to Dan. A corpse? I asked myself. No, presently this black-robed holy man began to say some words, and when Dan answered him in their language, he chatted a blue streak. (Why blue? You must explain this usage to me when we meet.)

"What does he say?" I asked Dan when the Buddhist monk seemed to have dozed off.

"He is full of pills," Dan answered me.

We had been conversing in our usual school English, so I was surprised when this Buddhist gentleman interrupted us in cultural language, probably learned in a foreign school.

"Not pills," he corrected. *"Pellets.* Have you not heard of 'cluster bombs'? What is your name, sir?"

"Nishina Shinzo, honored master, from Nagasaki. You refer to Lazy Dog maybe?" I asked.

"To C.B.U. in general," answered the well informed gentleman. "Lazy Dog bomb was followed by 'pineapple' type terror bomb and that was followed by 'guavas.' Guava is the name of mother bomb whose womb carries eight hundred steel pellets, sir."

The monk got interrupted by a scream from one of the guava children.

"Ah, here you can see final result of today's billion-dollar science," he said, after covering his eyes for an instant. "Scientists invent these annihilation weapons in luxury laboratories, returning at night to happy wives, well-fed children. While *our* children. . . ." The monk pointed at the weeping boy, who was as full of steel pellets as a pillow is full with rice. "The moral degeneration of science and of scientists everywhere is one of the saddest aspects of our time," he told me. But then he stopped talking again. "Ao-u," he moaned softly.

"Pains? A little fruit juice, honored *sensi?*" I inquired.

"No, it would be wasted on me. I think I shall soon be dead. If I do live on, I shall pour kerosene on myself, then light a match. Such protests give courage to our people to carry on their fight," the monk told me.

All at once I saw pained distress in his eyes. He was gazing at my drawing of our happy Japanese home, tacked above Dan's head.

"No one may dream of homes or other personal happiness until justice and peace come to our earth," said the monk solemnly. "We must all battle for that justice and that peace. Ao-u" he groaned again, even softer, and he closed his eyes.

Well, I too have the habit of closing my eyes when I do not wish people to see my expression. I took my glance discreetly from the monk and set it on Dan, who lay gazing at a comic parrot bird I have added to our drawing. (Dan had a green parrot, name of Pin, when she was a small Dan in her Honorable Grandfather's village, and she has been longing for such a bird ever since.) But now Dan's forehead was worried. Had my girl overheard that monk telling me we should not think of a happy home until everyone can have a peaceful home? Perhaps Dan would not come with me to Japan?

*"Dan!"* I cried with panic. "What?" she asked. "No, nothing," I murmured, but I began kissing her—her hand and her little ears. Finally her lips, which answered mine. I was happy again. Was that wrong, Mlle? My feeling happy, I mean, in that house of pain. But I have had so little happiness in my life.

Meanwhile black night had come down. I drew Dan into my arms.

*Nen nen koro ri.*
*Nen koro ron,*
*Nen koro ron.*

I sang this Japanese lullaby to Dan and soon "nen" (sleep) came over my girl. Mlle, I love her! Yes, I love her! Just then a cup of moonlight spilled through a hole in the roof over the honorable monk. Ha! He was sitting with his legs beneath him, his arms crossed, and on his wounded face was the classical "smiling Buddha" expression. A fine creature! Velvet outside, iron within. I loved him too.

Well, cheerio.
Shinzo

Dear Mlle,

Can you make out what I write, Mlle? Why do I
ask this? Because I am writing to you from a cave which
is as dark as those Nagasaki craters where I sat chewing
a half-roasted mouse after our great holocaust. And now
I have been holocausted again! Twenty-two years later
they returned to finish me off.

B-A-N-G!

Am I having a nightmare? I asked my half-asleep
self four nights ago. I jumped from my straw mat and
stared into the dark. I could see nothing, nobody. Suddenly I became eight years old again, lying before Gentle Jesus' church in Nagasaki, peering around for my
Honorable Mother and Father who had wafted off in a
flash of fire.

"Dan! Issa! Where are you?" I shouted, just as I
had shouted on That Day, "Mother-Father, where are
you?" And I heard myself continuing to shout in an
insane way, "Dan, Issa! Dan-Issa, where are you?"

I took two steps forward and fell flat over a body
robed in black. The monk! Yes, it was that fine fellow,
and I realized in horror that the bang—whatever it was
—had killed not only the man but also his hard-like-
steel will, his high education, his shining dreams. His

black robe was on fire. So our monk didn't have to pour kerosene on himself! They had done it for him, the burners. The flames lit up his face, and will you believe it? It still bore the expression of the "smiling Buddha."

"Dan-Dan!" I shouted again.

My frightened eyes moved toward our mat, and I could make out her slender body in the light of those flames that were eating the monk. A curl of blood had formed itself on Dan's forehead. Oh, what had hit her? I thought. A tile? Yes, a tile, no doubt. The whole roof seemed to have disappeared, and when I looked up I could see the stars.

Oh Mlle, I flung myself on Dan, and felt for her breast. Where was Dan's heart? Had it stopped? No, it hadn't! I began to weep noisily, and I understood then how big had become my love for Dan.

Water, I said to myself. Where is water? Well, nearly the whole shelter had been destroyed, but Dan's and my earthenware bowl stood there unbroken. So I poured water from said bowl over Dan's wound, and she opened her eyes. She looked at me with the kind of love that wasn't gratitude. It was a woman's love for a man. Ah, we clung together!

Now I will tell you something strange, Mlle. On that holocaust night, Dan and I became man and wife for the first time. Surrounded by dead, by dying, we felt a hot longing for life. Perhaps we wanted to create so that our species should not vanish. Mlle, can you understand that? No matter. No matter if the outside world understands, we doomed ones understand our own actions. And as we loved one another amidst the shrieks of the wounded, Dan and I understood life as never before. At this moment a little infant may be taking shape in Dan's flower-like body. Our own baby at last?

Later that night I stumbled my way through the ruins. Fallen stones and wood beams covered many bodies. A bleeding arm, a footless leg stuck out from the rubble. It was then, Mlle, that I learned the real meaning of hatred. As I stood among young people and helpless oldsters murdered wholesale and on purpose so as to spread terror among Asians, I promised myself never to stop hating for a moment, never to stop planning for revenge. The Buddhist monk had told me that enemy pilots have orders to aim at hospitals and schools, as this would break the Vietnam people's will of resistance. How wrong they are! Ah, Mlle, they have created for themselves such a store of hatred in the world that even their children and grandchildren will perish by its fire. Those burns will be as fatal for them as napalm and radiation have been fatal for us.

Respectfully,
Shinzo

Vietnam,

May –

Dear Mlle,

I never thought I would make my home inside a cave. But then would I have believed it possible, at age of seven, that next year I would live amongst ruins, eating garbage? However, my childhood ruins are old hat. This Vietnam cave is a new hat!

Well, everyone knows what a cave is like, and this cave is just like that—a damp dark hole with nervous bats. When I helped Issa carry Dan and five other survivors to above-mentioned abode, I thought we'd stay a day. A week has crawled by! One of the survivors got crazy and fled, and the two boys who set out to rescue him haven't returned. Devoured by beasts? Or caught, interrogated, tortured by other—beasts? The two remaining oldsters no longer eat. Fever is consuming them. I wash them with water which I gather from drops dripping from the roof, and I love them very much. My Dan, too, eats almost nothing. She can't get down the scraps Issa brings us at night.

Yes, I have to force this confession out of myself, Dan is very sick. The tough journey here sicked her body, the brutal bombardment sicked her soul. Only one month ago she was bombed in the hospital where she first lay, this also with a red cross painted on the roof.

And now again! Well, one thing can be said for our filthy cave: it has no red cross markings to draw their bombs. Hospitals, leper sanatariums, insane asylums and like pitiful places are their "priority targets." They won't waste their ammunition on a cave.

Mlle, how can I cheer my wife who contains little baby, maybe? In the old shelter I could add to my drawing of our Nagasaki home. Dan loved that. I had added a garden table where she could study her algebra, and had fitted a funny tail to her parrot, Pin. Dan smiled at said comic strips, and if I made a particularly silly addition, I could even make her laugh. I drew their water buffalo sitting down at table with the family to eat his supper, and Dan laughed and laughed. Oh, she must have been a gay Dan once!

But here I have neither scraps of paper nor pencils to draw pictures of our future life. This morning I had a good idea, however. One of the oldsters hemorrhaged, later in the day died, bad luck. I dipped a stick in a pool of his blood and began to draw some bold strokes on the cave wall. From holes in the roof light fell on my painting, but I could not finish peaceful cherry tree with Dan and our baby beneath it. Suddenly all the hatred inside me rushed into my fingers, and stopped my hand from making falsely happy picture.

So I dipped my stick again in the sacrificed blood and painted a burning city. Nagasaki perhaps, or a Vietnam city, or a city in other parts of the world which one day will be a target for *their* hatred. Above the city I painted men dropping atom bombs, dropping fire bombs, dropping high explosive bombs, dropping anti-personnel bombs. Yes, I painted the future, for they have sworn to bomb all their enemies wherever they are—that is every person, soldier or civilian, who cries out for peace and a better life.

Mlle, what do you think future generations will make of my "cave drawings"? In famous caves in Europe drawings remain made by primitive man, showing wild animals, man's worst enemy at that time. When beholding *my* crumbling paintings, executed in human blood, a hundred or a thousand years from now, people will be flabbergasted to learn that man's worst enemy in our time was—MAN. Yes, man himself! Oh, I long for a gentle tiger!

Yours respectfully, with horror,
Shinzo

Vietnam,
May –

Dear Mlle,

How are you tonight in your hotel room where we became good friends? I realize now what you celebrated when we drank saké together. Your great generosity that day made you a new person and we drank saké to that new person. Mlle, I like you.

"Man!" Issa cried as he rushed into our cave last night. His eyes seemed on fire, "We're leaving for the front at dawn. I'll call for you at daybreak with our film equipment," he added, while I took a step backward in dismay. After throwing a glance full of meaning in Dan's direction, my eyes telegraphed to Issa the following SOS: "I can't leave my sick wife." But Issa's determined face grew grim.

"You *must* leave! They are increasing their bombing. You and I must not be killed before our film is done. We don't count, man. The film does! We shall leave at six o'clock. O.K.?"

"Yes, O.K."

Now gently Issa kneeled beside Dan's mat. He gazed down at her, and his eyes began to weep. Oh, this Issa, Mlle—he is a very soft person inside.

"I got you a paw-paw," he told Dan. "I've juiced it

for you," he murmured, trying to make her drink the juice he'd brought her in his own little tin mug.

Bad luck, my girl could not drink. Dan can hardly swallow anything any more. However, I consumed hungrily the rice ball Issa had brought me. I peered at him over my rice ball, and saw his gaze rest on my "cave drawings" of Man annihilating Man.

"Shall we let *them* bring down the world to this?" Issa said, pointing at said drawings.

"What do you want to say?" I interrogated him.

"Well, the burners *must* be stopped! And the time is now. The place is here, in Vietnam. We must help halt them, man. You will have to make the greatest sacrifice of your life."

"Leaving my . . . ?" I began.

Issa nodded, then bent down and leaned his forehead against Dan's mat for some seconds. He sprang to his feet. The glance he gave my poor fever-shaking girl was so full of pity that I iced. Issa had beheld hundreds of napalmers, and he saw that Dan will never get well, that she will never leave her straw mat. Reading this judgment in his eyes, I died for the second time in twenty-two years. Ah, Mlle, Gentle Jesus from Nagasaki was wrong: men *do* know what they are doing! I have learned this.

"Please leave us, Issa," I told my friend. "I shall be ready for you at dawn," I added in Japanese, and Issa hurried from our shelter without a backward glance. He was as white as a paper sheet, Mlle.

On this note I terminate, signing myself yours in appreciation,

Shinzo

P.S. If possible will write you a little say good-bye note before leaving at sunrise.

Vietnam,
May –

Goodbye Mlle,

Here comes the goodbye-for-now note I promised to write, time permitting. Dawn and Issa will be here in ten minutes, so excuse bad penmanship which I scorn, if you please.

Well, after Issa had run off into the night, I kneeled on Dan's mat and stayed there for hours, thinking. Dan's eyes were closed, and she was asleep, or half asleep. Suddenly she opened her eyes, that were like black velvet from fever. She smiled at me dazedly.

"I was dreaming," she said. "Of Pin. He was hanging upside down in his tree, whistling."

I kissed that brow that always was full of poetic images, and I felt grateful that her delirium-dreams were happy. My wife was so weak that she could scarcely keep her long-lashed eyes open, and yet she looked at ease. Perhaps the memory of her childhood parrot had brought her back to the village of her Honorable Grandparents in the peaceful rice paddies. Ha! A lucky time for my decision! From the lining of my black Vietnamese jacket I took out the tissue paper with the precious object inside. When above-mentioned round object dropped in Dan's paw-paw juice it made no splash, no ripple.

"Drink, my Dan."

Dan shook her round, sweet head. It hurt her to swallow.

I pleaded: "For *my* sake, Dan," the way one does with a sick child who must take medicine.

Then her eyes sent me all the love that I have never had before. Now I will have it always!

And then she drank. I lay quietly down beside my wife, holding her hand in an eternity-clasp. At first Dan gave me back the pressing of my fingers, but all at once her body convulsed. My pill was doing its work of love. Yes! Poison is the only kind thing in a world where men burn men, like *they* burned us in Nagasaki and now again here in Vietnam. Oh, good pill, poison pill, you are my friend! While I was thinking this, I stroked my darling's hair.

"Are you—asleep, Dan? Already? Then I am happy. No one can throw fire at you. No one can scar you, mutilate you any more. You are safe at last, like no living person in the whole world is safe. Dan. . . . Dan. . . .